Eamonn the Mighty

Zipper Club Warrior

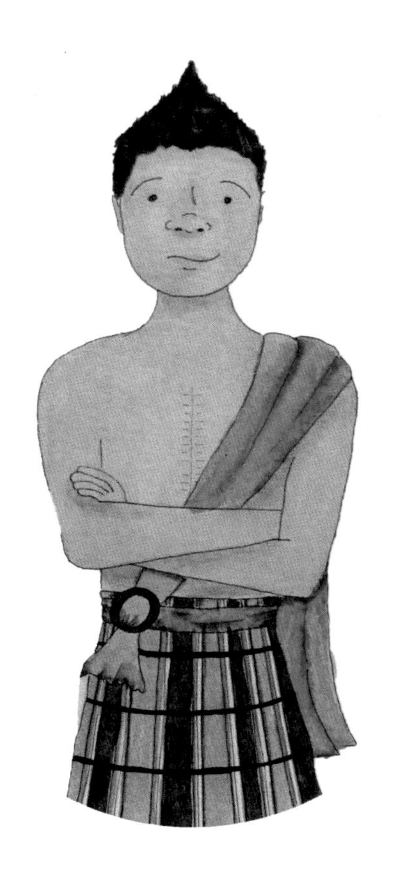

Written and Illustrated by Kristen Moran

For those unfamiliar with the name, “Eamonn” is pronounced “ay” + “mun”

ISBN-13: 978-1-7290-7502-9

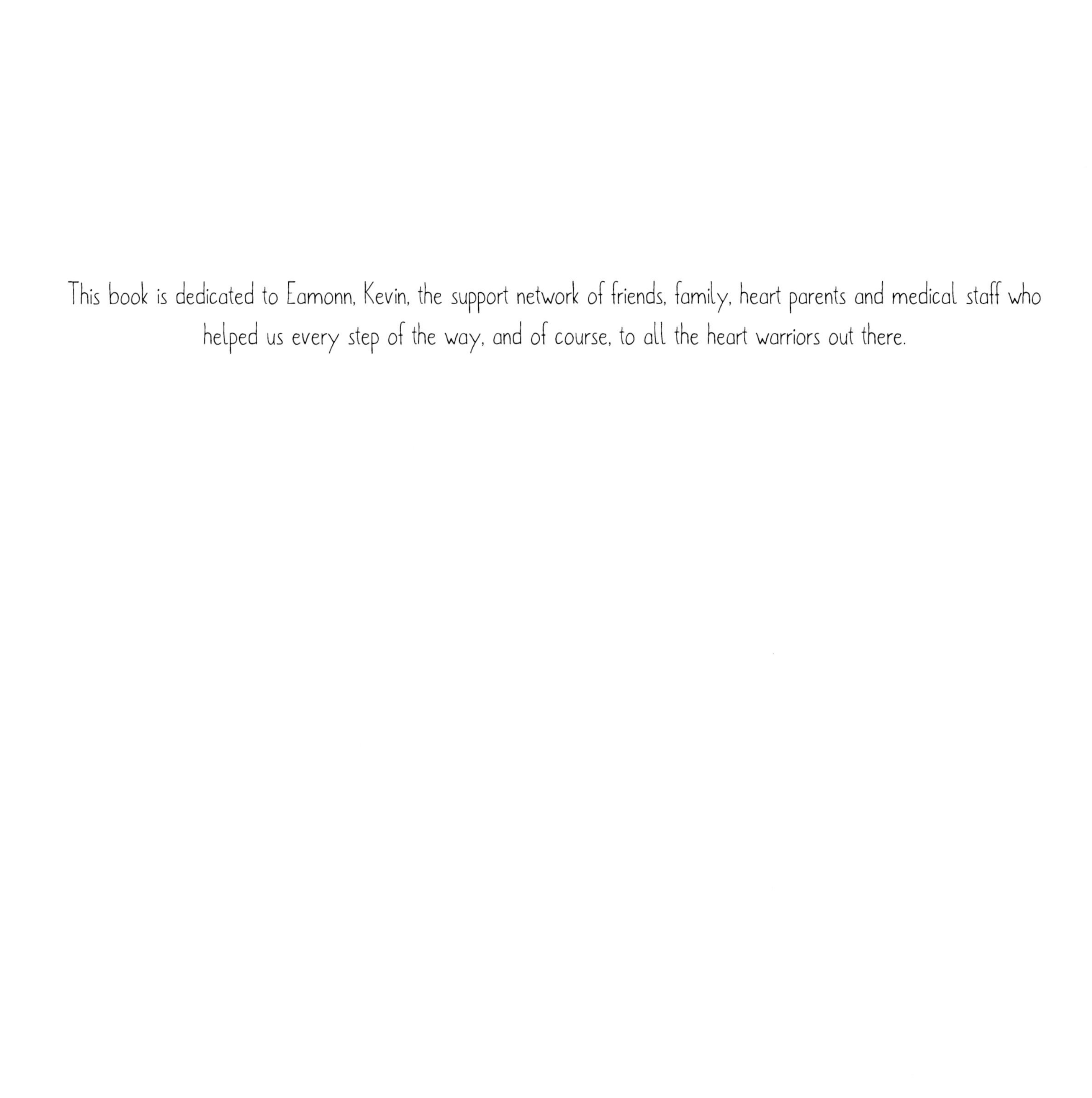

This book is dedicated to Eamonn, Kevin, the support network of friends, family, heart parents and medical staff who helped us every step of the way, and of course, to all the heart warriors out there.

There once was a warrior
so brave and so bold,
whose story's the greatest
that's ever been told.

He's Eamonn the mighty
with the heart of a fighter.
Settle in as I tell you
how he made his town's future brighter.

The Cold Hearted Dragon,
they called CHD,
was terrorizing the village
by land and by sea.

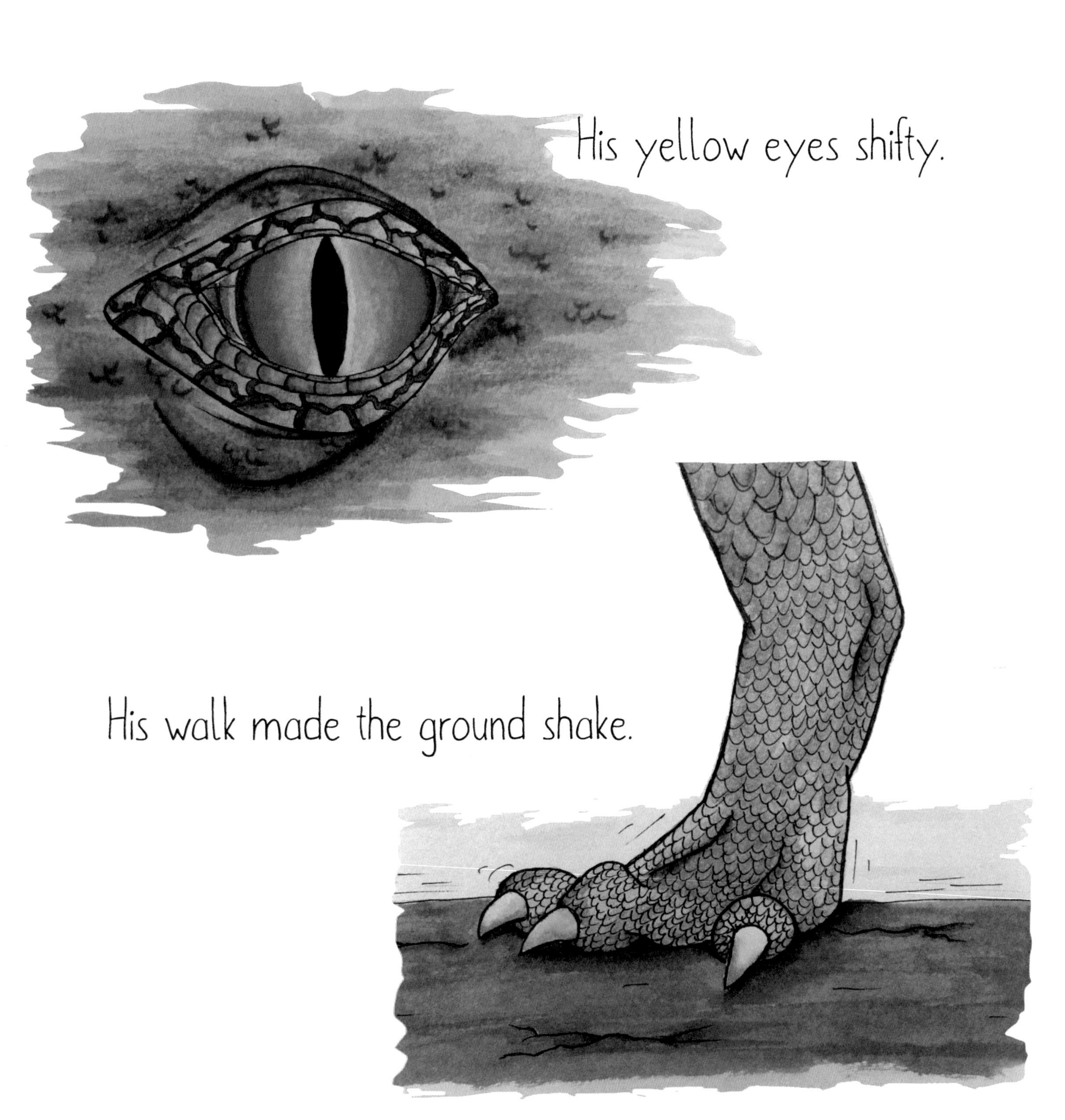
His yellow eyes shifty.
His walk made the ground shake.

His breath's made of fire,

leaving fear in his wake.

But how could the village
beat him once and for all?
That's when Eamonn stood up
ready to answer the call.

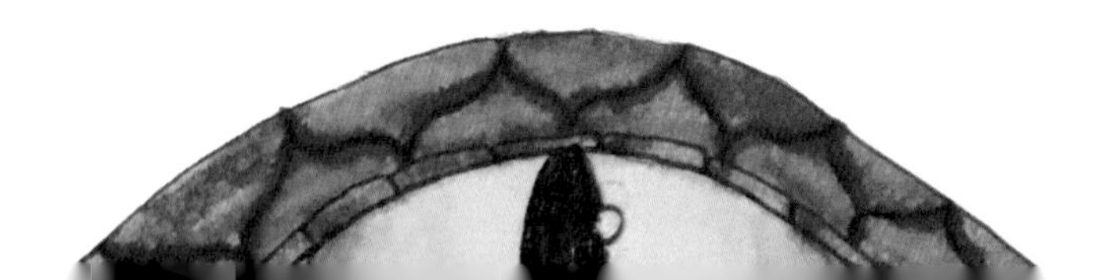
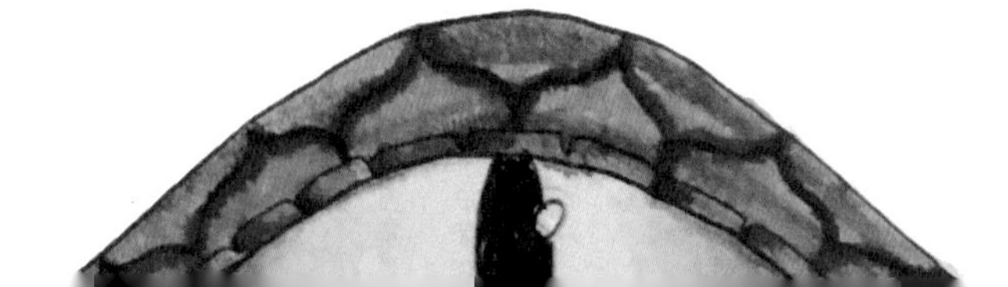

"I can stop him!" he exclaimed.
"I'll take this no more!

CHD doesn't scare me,

not his SIZE,

not his ROAR."

"I'll need all the courageous,
the strong, and the clever.
Won't you all join me in defeating CHD forever?"

The warriors were gathered
to hear Eamonn's plan.
"If anyone can do it,
I am certain we can!"

When all of a sudden
from up in the clouds

appeared the Cold Hearted Dragon
ready to descend on the crowds.

Eamonn grabbed his sword swiftly.
The warriors followed his lead.
They all fought bravely
determined to succeed.

As the dragon attacked,
his claws struck their chests.
Yet they never relented
on their arduous quest.

The warriors were victorious.
The dragon was slayed.
Their chest scars healed like zippers
and so history was made.

The End

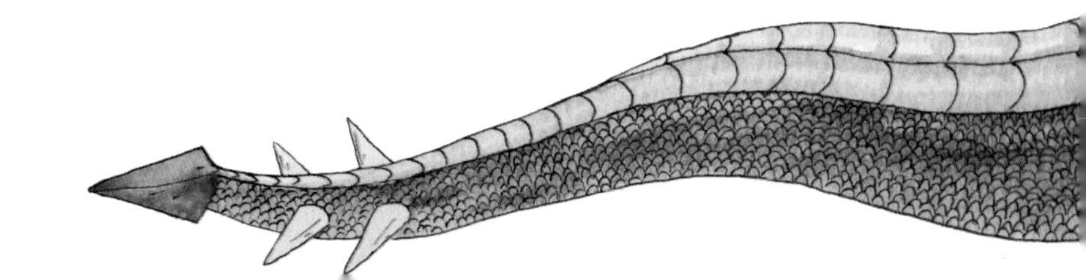

"Never be ashamed of a scar. It simply means you are stronger than whatever tried to hurt you."

- *Anonymous*

Eamonn, this is for you.

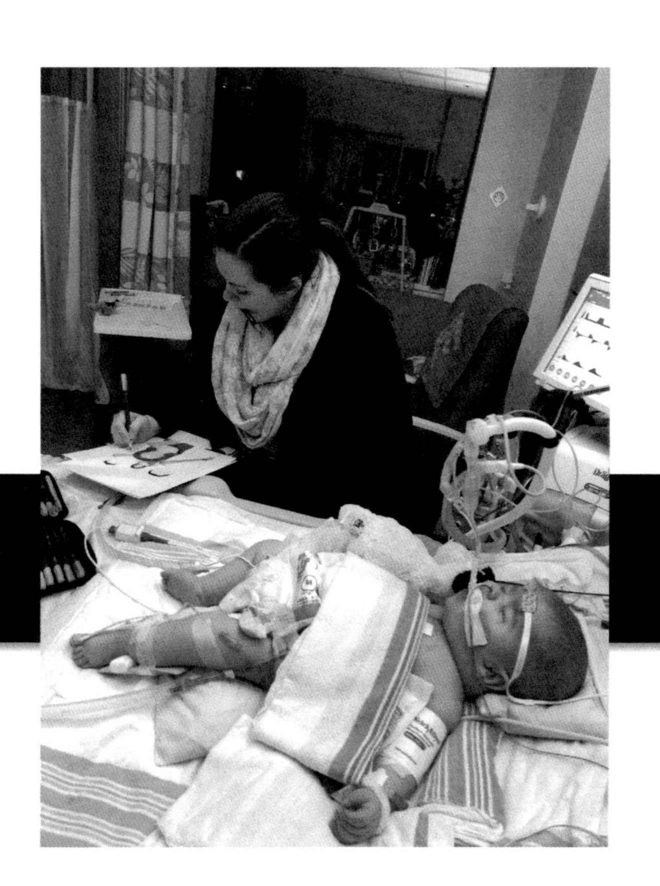

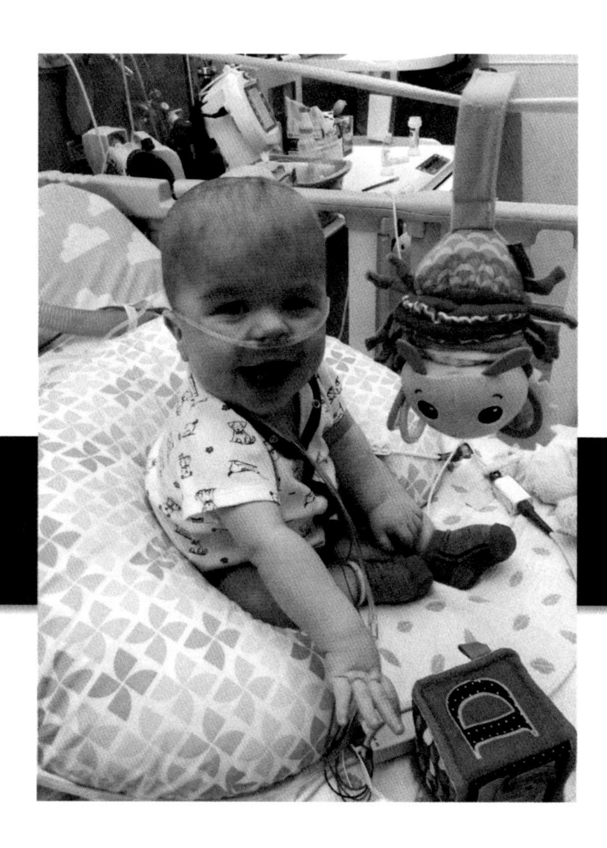

From the moment you were born, you inspired me with your strength, determination, perseverance, and constant desire to learn and grow despite having undergone five heart surgeries, including your transplant, all before your first birthday. You are the definition of a warrior. You are my light and my hero. I love you immensely. Forever and always.

Made in the USA
Middletown, DE
11 July 2021